THE PSEUDONYM'S BRIDE

A SHORT MYSTERY

ALEXANDRIA BLAELOCK

Also by Alexandria Blaelock

SHORT STORY COLLECTIONS
The Haunting of Hayward Hall
Lovelorn, Lovestruck and Love at First Sight
Common or Garden Variety Heroes
Case Files of the Wilkinson Detective Agency

FICTION
That Love Nonsense

MS BLAELOCK'S BOOKS
Stress Free Dinner Parties
Signature Wardrobe Planning
Holistic Personal Finance
Minimally Viable Housekeeping
Planning a Life Worth Living

A SELECTION OF AVAILABLE SHORT STORIES
Alma's Grace
Balancing the Book
Bygone Boyfriend
Fate in Your Hands
Kiss of Death
Lady of the Looking Glass
Life in the Security Directorate
Love in the Security Directorate
Morning Star, Evening Star, Superstar
Needy Bitch
Payton's Run
Secret Singer
Shining Star
Ship in a Bottle
Simone Says Hands in the Air
The Day the Schedule Broke

THE PSEUDONYM'S BRIDE

A SHORT MYSTERY

ALEXANDRIA BLAELOCK

BlueMere Books
MELBOURNE, AUSTRALIA

For permission requests, please contact
enquiries@bluemerebooks.com.

Ordering Information:
Discounts are available on quantity purchases. For details, contact orders@bluemerebooks.com.

The Pseudonym's Bride/Alexandria Blaelock
paperback ISBN: 978-1-925749-76-2
digital ISBN: 978-1-925749-77-9

THE PSEUDONYM'S BRIDE

Celeste stood on the verandah, hot coffee in hand. The sun was just peeping above the horizon, painting the sky orange while a light mist shrouded the dying lawn in mystery. A pair of magpies warbled from the bare branch of a nearby dead tree.

It looked like the start of a beautiful Spring day. Almost too good to spend pulling apart the old cottage. Though she looked forward to the day it was gone forever.

She shuddered reflexively and changed her focus to observe it in all its squat, ugly glory.

They'd first inspected the property two years ago to the day. She and Dash had stood, appalled, in front of the cottage for the longest time. He'd looked at her, and the immense doubt she'd felt was clearly written all over her face.

He'd taken her hand, brought it to his lips, and kissed it tenderly.

"It's not so bad. It's functional, liveable, and there's plenty of space to build the exact character cottage you want out the back.

"And your beautiful garden." He gestured an arm wildly to the east, "Your labyrinth can go over there," followed by a gesture to the west, "and the reflecting pool could go over there in that grove of gum trees."

She'd shrugged one shoulder and looked at him out of the corner of her eye. It seemed like rather too much work.

He'd gently turned her south to face the industrial unit, "and there's this..."

"This" was the big drawcard. A small industrial unit on the street frontage containing two private offices, an open office come reception area and a small warehouse at the rear. Nicely fenced off from the residential side of the property.

All set up and ready to move into - nothing to stop them spreading out and getting the business up and running at the next level.

She'd turned to face the cottage again. If anything, it was the deal-breaker. Tiny, dark, and reeking of despair.

Of their own volition, her hands had waved in dismissal at it. "But... But... Just look at it. It's grotesque! It doesn't look like it's been updated or redecorated since it was built a hundred and fifty years ago."

"I'm sure it's not that old.

"I know it's not much to look at now, but cut back those shrubs to let some light in, open the windows to let in some air - it'll be fine.

"It'll be like glamping.

"And it'll only be six months hon," he smiled, "a year tops."

But anyone who knows anything about construction projects knows you need double the time and triple the cost. If you're lucky, the bank won't cut off your credit, and if you're not, they'll take everything you own.

The new house had walls now, a roof and lockable doors. They'd moved all their things up the night before and slept on the floor because they were too tired to unpack and put things away.

The power and water were connected, but without a functional bathroom and kitchen, Council wouldn't give them an Occupancy Certificate approving the building for habitation.

And without the Occupancy Certificate, the bank wouldn't release any further funding.

Which was complicated, because without that additional funding, she couldn't install the kitchen or bathrooms.

And without the kitchen and at least one bathroom, the property was essentially industrial, and wouldn't sell for enough to cover the debt.

And if that wasn't bad enough, the bank was threatening to call in not only the housing loan, but the business's line of credit too.

Which was, of course, secured by a property valued for a house that wasn't yet finished.

Not to mention almost fully extended.

The good old Construction Catch-22.

She sighed, what they really needed was a miracle.

She swallowed the last of her cold coffee in a gulp, collected together her tool kit and supplies, and left the house.

During the start-stop-start-stop of the building project, she'd had plenty of time to work on the garden, constructing the basic foundations of a drought tolerant Mediterranean style garden.

Gravel paths wended their maze-like way through raised vegetable beds and concealed water tanks, tall terracotta pots housing cypress topiary, and covered archways.

She'd been fortunate that debris from the initial site works for the industrial unit hadn't been cleared away, so much of the garden materials had been scavenged from the property.

Wheelbarrow load by wheelbarrow load.

She walked through the garden, brushing her free hand through the fragrant lavender and rosemary bushes.

She'd fondly imagined drinking chilled wine while eating her own preserves on seats nestled in secluded nooks throughout the garden.

Her home, a sanctuary, a secret hideaway from the hustle and bustle of life.

But now, despite the garden's tranquillity, it seemed more like an oppressive burden she couldn't get out from under.

Dash was no help. The dynamic go-getter she'd married had been ground down by the difficulties they'd faced until he was just a useless shell of his former self.

Not only had he stopped taking care of the business, but of himself as well, childlike in his insistence on lying on the bare, uncovered floor, eating chips and playing computer games on the television.

Now and again, she'd catch him watching daytime television instead.

Like a useless fat slug.

She was trying to run the business, build the house, and look after her suddenly infantile husband, but she didn't know how much longer she could keep going.

Except maybe forever, because she didn't have a choice. Their safety net was so full of holes that if she gave up now, they'd lose everything.

She'd lose everything, because doing without Dash was beginning to look better than doing with him.

On her way to the old cottage, she checked the water was turned off at the junction, then turned the power off and removed the fuses.

Thank goodness they'd had the foresight to put in separate lines for the new construction.

The cottage was as tiny and dark as ever, despite the initial effort they'd put into cheering it up. Summer or winter, it had been cold and damp inside. Windows open or closed, it had smelled musty and mouldy.

It felt sometimes as though the cottage had fallen into a deep depression after losing its first owner and never recovered.

Not content with a top note of despair, it had added despondency and desperation to its final fragrance formulation.

But the antique fittings she'd derided on their first viewing were a godsend now she needed them to "finish" the house.

In terms of living conditions, they were fine because the industrial unit included a fully equipped kitchen and bathroom; whatever happened, they'd be OK for cooking and eating.

The real urgency was maximising the potential price in case the bank foreclosed.

With that in mind, she'd spent the previous evening in her office watching YouTube videos of kitchen and bathroom demolitions, and felt reasonably confident she had the required tools and could disconnect the fixtures in a day.

In an excess of positivity, she'd booked a plumber and electrician for the next day, gambling she could bully Dash into helping her wheelbarrow the pieces up there.

In an ideal universe, she'd have sent them away to be re-enamelled, but there wasn't the time or money for that, so she'd be giving them a hard scrub with a wire brush when she got them out, and hopefully a lick of enamel paint before they were installed.

Of if the worst came to the worst, after.

Given how bad their luck had been since they bought the property, she offered a small prayer for safety to whatever deity might be listening before stepping over the threshold.

Her safety booted footsteps echoed dully in the empty building.

She thought the kitchen might be the easier of the two rooms to demolish, with the potential to get it done in a couple of hours, so she carried her tool kit in there.

It was too quiet, so she turned on her smartphone, tapped the local radio station app, and linked it with her Bluetooth speaker for some background noise.

The light didn't come on when she flicked the switch, and the water sputtered and quickly ran out when she tried the tap.

It seemed safe to get going.

The first step was to remove the stove, a forty or fifty-year-old, standalone electric upright, which was just a matter of unplugging it and dragging it out of the way.

It was partly stuck to the floor with cooking fat, and Celeste had to rock it backwards and forwards a few times to get enough momentum to get it moving, but despite that, it was straightforward.

She pushed and pulled it out the back door, and left it at the edge of the utility area where it would be easy to get at to move later.

A good start.

She took her water bottle from her tool kit, turned to look at the sink as she took a long drink.

It was the original enamelled iron sink, the kind with a built-in splashback that's hung off the wall and rests on a matching stand.

She got out her torch and took a good look under the sink, but couldn't tell if it was bolted to the wall, or just hanging off a mount.

The pipe connections were old and rusty, but with her trusty adjustable long handled spanner, she managed to undo the joins without breaking anything.

Given the number of false starts and slips, she was grateful to be wearing long, thick cotton sleeves and heavy-duty gloves. She'd hardly started, and it was already looking like a good day to splurge on takeout for dinner.

Remembering the time she lost her wedding ring down the drain, she carefully removed the U-bend and put it in a bucket to check later.

She leaned on the sink to see how movable it was, and it stood firm. She shoved it a few times, and it remained firm.

Hard to know whether that was gravity, rust or that the parts were fixed together. Regardless it was bloody heavy, and even if she could get it apart, would difficult to move.

But more or less ready to move it was.

The tiny kitchen didn't have proper built-in cupboards, only a collection of open wooden boxes that might once have been fruit crates held together with paint and nailed to the wall.

They had a certain retro charm, and were still in reasonably serviceable condition, so Celeste decided to try removing them on the principle that some storage was better than no storage.

Starting with the base cabinets, she grabbed a thin pry bar and edged it behind the first box. Applying a little force, she eased it just off the wall, managing not to damage it or the wall.

Perhaps the cottage was more resilient than she first thought.

Encouraged, she decided to try and remove the collection as one unit rather than a box at a time. She moved the pry bar a little further along the wall, carefully seesawing it along the wall until the unit was loosened.

As she stepped back to survey her work, she heard the wood scream as it pulled free from the nails, and leapt forward to catch the unit as it fell from the wall.

But she couldn't catch it all; some of it hit the floor and broke apart, and she was left holding a box in the middle of a pile of kindling.

It was too much.

She fell to her knees, cradling the box and gasped hard, guttural sobs as the tears fought to escape from her eyes.

How had her life come to this?

This property was supposed to be their launching pad, not their destruction.

Somehow, she'd managed to control her fear and focus on just the very next thing.

Somehow, she'd just kept putting one foot in front of the other, and what was it all for?

The business was dying.

Her marriage was dying.

Her hope was dying.

Maybe it was just time to call it quits. Take the loss and move on.

Could anything be worse than sitting in the godforsaken cottage in a pile of wood chips worrying about when the bank was going to foreclose?

Worrying about how to pay the mountain of bills.

Worrying about when Dash was going to snap out of it.

She wished she had a cigarette. And a decade after quitting, she wished she could afford to buy a packet.

What the fuck was it all for?

«« • »»

Some time later, she carefully set the box aside and stood up. She took her gloves off, dropping them on the floor, then poured some water on her lucky bandanna and wiped her face with it.

Repeating the country club's last call, she told the room "Ding, ding. Time, gentlemen time."

Her words fell to the floor like stones.

She kicked the remains of the cabinets out of her way as she headed out the door.

Then she remembered her phone, and swearing, turned to pick it up.

And saw the falling cabinets had torn the layers of ancient linoleum back and broken through the rotten floorboards. Some of the boards had dissolved into dust revealing a suspiciously uneven dirt floor.

Suspicious in that there was the kind of dip in the ground that TV detectives usually agreed meant a decomposed body.

Celeste retrieved a glove, pulling it on as she tested a joist with her foot. It didn't give much, so she knelt on it and scooped some of the dirt in the dip aside.

It wasn't long before she came across some bones.

She thought they might be fingers.

She stood and backed away from the hole.

Clearly not an emergency situation, so she grabbed her phone, and after a quick search for the number of her local police station, gave them a call.

"I'm doing some work on an old cottage, and I've found a skeleton."

"Sorry ma'am, did you say you've found a skeleton."

"Yes officer, it's under the floor. I think it's human."

"What's the address."

She gave them the address

"Ma'am, please leave the building. Don't do anything further, just leave everything exactly as it is and wait outside. Officers are on the way."

"Thank you."

Celeste took the water, but left her tools and went outside.

It was an irritating delay in progress, and she wondered what the bank might think. Though it was too soon to get too stressed about that.

The remains might not be human.

The police might laugh at her and leave.

She might still be able to gut the cottage before nightfall.

Luckily, she didn't have long to worry. The marked car arrived so quickly she felt they could almost have been watching the place waiting for her to find the body.

Two uniformed officers approached her.

"Ms Baillieu?"

She nodded.

"I'm Officer Ellison, and this is Officer Lewis. You called because you believe you've found some human remains?"

She nodded.

"Would you please show us where you found them?"

She led the way into the kitchen and indicated the broken floorboards.

The officers nodded at each other, and Lewis drew her back outside, turning her around so she couldn't see into the cottage.

He took out his notebook, "would you please tell me who you are and what you were doing when you found the remains?"

She quickly outlined buying the property, building the house while living in the cottage, and now gutting it to move the fittings up to the house.

"And is the kitchen the only room you've worked on?"

"Yes sir, the rest is structurally as it was when we purchased the property."

"And when you say us, you mean your husband?"

She thought she heard Ellison talking in the cottage, and strained her ears, trying to hear what was going on.

"Ms Baillieu." Lewis prompted. She blinked and brought her attention back to him.

"Sorry. Yes sir, Dashiell Baillieu, my husband. Though he hasn't been well and hasn't done any work on the cottage recently."

Hopefully she could keep him out of this. God knew what it might do to him on top of everything else.

Weirdly, it had given her something else to think about, and in a roundabout way, her sanity back.

Ellison rejoined them.

"Ms Baillieu, I've examined the bones, and it appears they're human. I've put in a call to forensics, and they'll be here shortly.

"That means this is now a crime scene, and you are no longer permitted to enter the building until we've finished our investigation. Do you understand?"

"Yes ma'am. Can we use the other buildings, or do we have to find somewhere else to stay?"

"Other buildings?"

Celeste took a few steps along the path, and pointed uphill to the house, "We've just moved in up there," she pointed downhill to the office, "and we work down there."

The officers looked at each other, Lewis shrugged, and Ellison said, "that will probably be fine, but we'll need forensics to confirm."

Ellison took her arm. "You appear to be bleeding, perhaps you'd allow us to offer first aid while we wait?"

She looked down at her arm and noticed for the first time the blood soaking through a tear in her work shirt. She swayed a little, and Lewis caught her as she staggered.

They escorted her to a nearby tree stump, where she sat. Lewis waited with her while Ellison retrieved a first aid kit from the car.

By the time her arm had been cleaned and bandaged, a forensics team had arrived and started assembling their kit. Lewis went to greet them, and returned with a young woman while Ellison led the rest of the team into the cottage.

The young woman asked her to repeat her story about discovering the remains while taking a DNA swab and scanning her fingerprints. Though Celeste didn't see how her DNA could get anywhere near a skeleton who'd been there for God knows how long.

The woman also confirmed they had the run of the house and office, but must stay beyond the police tape perimeter Ellison was putting up. Then she went into the cottage, and Lewis went to assist Ellison.

Another car pulled up and disgorged more people, presumably detectives.

Even though it was probably the remains of a human being, and they were buried under a cottage, did it really merit this much attention?

Surely, it'd been there for decades. Probably not long enough to be archaeology, but what were they expecting to find?

Celeste repeated her story once more for a man who introduced himself as Detective Shaw, who thanked her and walked into the cottage, leaving her alone.

She stood on the path, watching the people swarm over the cottage like enraged ants protecting their nest. She wasn't certain whether she'd been dismissed, or should wait for someone to tell her to go.

She sat back down on the stump and thought about what this might mean.

She'd naively assumed it would be barely a blip in her schedule, but it was beginning to look like a major roadblock.

Not content with the cottage interior, there were jumpsuited people examining the exterior walls and the ground, though she had no idea what they were expecting to find.

It was irritating not to be moving forward with her plan, but at the same time, an enforced break would give her more time to think strategically about their situation.

And to put some uninterrupted effort back into the business.

There was a shout from inside the cottage and a flurry of activity, but she had no clue what any of it meant.

Though it felt a lot like the kind of something important that meant they'd be around longer rather than shorter.

She sighed.

And then berated herself for not thinking about the dead person as more than an obstacle in her path.

Or for their family who'd probably been waiting for decades for news of their missing relative.

She scrubbed her face with her hands, and tried to think about what was next.

The good news was that they could stay in the house, and work in the office. The bad news was she'd have to cancel the plumber and electrician.

Should she phone the bank and let them know? Or leave it a few days and see what the police investigation had found?

There hadn't been a formal letter of demand, only an indication that they weren't prepared to release any further funds at this point.

One thing was certain, she was tired and filthy. Perhaps the best start was to go to the office and take a shower. Then she could nap for an hour or two and reassess the situation.

She caught Lewis's attention, telling him she was going to the office, and reminding him that Dash was unwell and asking that he be left alone.

«« • »»

The police tape remained in place for several weeks. She'd seen lights at night now and again, and more than once thought she'd heard some kind of machinery, but hadn't seen anything to confirm it.

Sometimes the old tape was replaced by new tape, and sometimes it seemed as though the area it enclosed got larger, though she couldn't say for sure.

She was surprised the police were still active on the scene. She'd expected they would have cleared out and taken their crime scene tape with them by now.

How long did it take to remove one skeleton?

And what did the cottage interior look like - was there anything left to salvage for the new house?

She'd left messages for Detective Shaw who hadn't called her back.

She'd tried questioning the people on the scene who claimed not to know anything.

Not knowing what was going on was frustrating.

She'd mentioned the police investigation to Dash, and he was surprisingly disinterested, barely interrupting his game to listen.

She'd made time to open the blinds and windows in her office, letting in the sunshine and fresh air. She'd tidied it up, stacking and rearranging the boxes, papers and samples into some kind of order.

Even her brain felt quicker and cleaner, as if she'd cleaned and defragmented its hard drive.

Lacking other distractions, she'd put some consistent effort into the business, and it had perked up a bit.

Money was coming in again.

In fact, she thought they were now in a position to draw some out some profits to finish one of the bathrooms at the house to a minimum standard.

Just as well given Dash couldn't be bothered coming down to the office to bathe, and the new house was starting to smell like a teenage boy's bedroom.

She decided to go home for lunch and share the news.

But there was no sign of him.

He wasn't in the house, and she couldn't see him in the garden.

The car was still parked under the carport.

It was possible he'd walked past while she was in the windowless warehouse packing orders, but she couldn't think why he'd do that without stopping in to see her.

Weird, but probably nothing to worry about.

As she walked back to the office, she noticed that the cottage was quiet, and wondered whether he'd broken the cordon to see what was happening in there.

She looked around to see if anyone was nearby, and not seeing anyone, ducked under the tape. After rubbing her suddenly sweaty hands down the legs of her jeans, she pushed the door open.

And wondered where the cottage had gone.

All that remained were the roof and external walls. No internal walls, no floorboards, only a well churned dirt floor, with plastic bags of dirt stacked around the walls.

Clearly the police had removed the interior, but for what possible reason?

Was it possible there had been more than one body under the floor?

Had she been eating, sleeping, and having sex on top of a bunch of dead bodies?

She put her hands on her mouth to hold the vomit in as she backed away from the door. Her eyes were wide and staring as her brain joined assorted dots and came up with answers she hoped were wrong.

She yelped as she backed into an unexpected obstruction, and spun around, half expecting something monstrous.

She was relieved to find it was just a dishevelled Detective Shaw, stinking of stale cigarette smoke.

She slapped a hand to her chest, "Detective, you startled me."

"Weren't you told to stay away from the cottage?"

"Yes, I was just looking for Dash."

"That would be Dashiell Baillieu, your husband?"

"Yes, I was just wondering what he wanted for lunch."

"And what does he want?"

"I'm, not sure, I haven't found him yet."

"Are you saying he's not on the property?"

"That's unlikely, but not impossible."

She scratched her forehead with a finger, "Detective, is there something wrong?"

He sighed and ran a hand through what was left of his hair. "Ms Baillieu, is there somewhere we can talk?"

Given the state of the house, she took him to the office, "can I get you some tea or coffee?"

"White coffee with one would be good."

His phone buzzed and he looked at it, "Actually Ms Baillieu, some new information has come in, would you mind coming with me to the station?"

"Am I under arrest?"

"Not at all, it's that there are some papers we need you to sign."

Celeste nodded, "fine, let's go then."

The Detective didn't say anything during the short drive, and despite her almost overwhelming curiosity, neither did she.

Being called into the station couldn't be better news than whatever he'd intended to tell her in her home.

She was shown into an interview room, and accepted the offer of a coffee, smiling slightly as she asked for "white with one."

Seated on her own for what seemed like forever, she examined the scuffed, dirty walls and floor, trying not to imagine what else might have taken place in the room.

She was about ready to run screaming from the room when he returned with coffee in both hands and a bunch of papers tucked under an armpit.

"Sorry to take so long Ms Baillieu."

Celeste shrugged one shoulder in reply as she reached for her coffee. "Would you please call me Celeste, you're making me feel like my mother-in-law, and that's not a good thing."

He grunted in reply as he fiddled in a nearby cupboard coming out with some paper and a pen.

"Ms... Sorry, Celeste. I've got some information to tell you about the cottage."

She nodded, just once.

"During the course of our investigation, we recovered the remains of six women, including a Mrs June Hammond, the previous owner of the property."

She gasped and opened her mouth to ask any one of the hundreds of questions that sprung to mind, but he raised a hand to forestall her.

"Let me just tell you what we know, and if you have any questions when I'm done, you can ask them then."

She nodded.

"Are you aware of Mrs Hammond?"

She shook her head. "No, Dash took care of all the purchasing particulars."

"Mrs Hammond was reported missing around three years ago, and we now know she was murdered around that time.

"We also know an application to declare her missing was lodged exactly the minimum 90 days after the initial missing persons report, and her nephew, a Mr Robert Daggett was appointed to control her financial affairs.

"Do you know anyone by this name?"

"No."

"I'm now going to show you pictures of the deceased women, and I'd like you to tell me if you recognise any of them."

He laid out the first picture, watching her reaction closely.

She gasped as she saw a young, smiling, square-faced blonde woman with blue eyes. A woman who looked a bit like her.

"Do you know this woman?"

No, I... I was just taken aback by our similarity."

He laid out a second photo of a young, square-faced blonde woman with blue eyes.

She looked up, searching his impassive face for some clue to what he was thinking.

He laid out a third. Then a fourth, and a fifth. All young, square-faced blonde women with blue eyes.

She shivered, "it looks like your killer has a type."

"Yes," he laid out another photo, "and this is Mrs Hammond."

An older, square-faced woman with faded blonde hair and blue eyes.

Celeste picked up the photo and looked closely at it, "she looks vaguely familiar, but I just can't place her right now. Maybe it's just that she's the same type as the others."

"Now I'm going to show you a picture of her nephew Mr Daggett, and I'd like to know if you recognise him."

He laid the picture on the desk with a snap.

Her chair scraped across the floor as she jumped back, looking at the picture as if it was an enormous cockroach running across the table towards her.

"That's not Daggett, that's my husband! That's Dashiell Baillieu."

Shaw nodded, it seemed, with satisfaction.

"I'm sorry to upset you Ms Baillieu, but I have some more questions. Do you feel you can continue?"

Celeste sat back down and reached for her coffee, taking a big gulp before she nodded. "Wait, do you have a cigarette?"

"This is a non-smoking building, but we can go out the back for a smoke if you like."

She nodded.

He led the way out, gesturing to one of his colleagues to follow them, standing discreetly in the doorway as Shaw tapped a cigarette loose from the pack and offered it to her.

She took it with a shaky hand, and after he'd lit it, took a deep drag. "It's funny that no matter how long since the last one, it's as if you never gave up."

"Yes," he replied, lighting one for himself. "Can you tell me how you met the man you call Baillieu?"

"In the University tavern, about, I don't know, five years ago?"

"Did you approach him, or did he approach you?"

"I don't know, it was a long time ago."

"That's not really true is it Celeste? All women can spin a romantic story about the first time they met their husbands."

She took another drag, "no, it's true. I was drunk and dating someone else when we first met. I don't remember. Dash told me he'd seen me around and decided he was going to marry me."

She retched as she realised what she'd said.

"Was he stalking me? Did he kill these women while he was stalking me?"

He regarded her steadily for a moment before answering, "yes. It certainly looks that way."

She retched again, and again. And before long the remains of her police station coffee were splattered on the ground beside her.

"But how..." she started.

"But how..." she tried again.

"How am I still alive? How are there six dead women under the cottage I was living in a few weeks ago? How is all this possible when he was living a perfectly ordinary life in my flat with me?"

"We were rather hoping you could tell us that Celeste."

"I'm going to be sick," she said, puking up more coffee and a bit of breakfast too.

"This is a nightmare. Where is Dash?"

"We have no records of Dashiell Baillieu. He doesn't exist."

"Of course he exists - I slept with him last night! I had breakfast with him this morning? What do you mean he doesn't exist?"

"We have security footage of the man you know as Dashiell Baillieu withdrawing a large amount of cash from his account at the Green Bank yesterday."

"That's not possible, he's been ill. He won't leave the house...

"And for that matter, we don't have any accounts at Green Bank."

"And where did you say he was when I found you?"

"I don't know," she whispered, "I don't know."

She looked up at the detective, "I don't know him at all, do I?"

"I don't think so."

"Has he killed anyone else?"

"We don't know for certain, but there are several missing women that fit his type."

It was then she realised that none of it mattered.

Not the house, the cottage or the business.

The bank could take it and sell it, and she would be better off without it.

"Why on earth did he buy the property if he knew it would come to this?"

"I don't know the answer to that, but maybe he thought it would be possible to conceal the remains for longer. Maybe forever."

"Am I next? Is he coming after me?"

"We don't know for sure." He gave her a lopsided smile, "it might be that your attempts to protect him from the investigation saved your life.

And given you had no reason to suspect or fear him up to now, it seems more likely he's absconded."

"What if he comes back? Will I be safe from him?"

"Is there anywhere else you can stay?"

"No, and I don't have enough money to stay somewhere else."

"We might be able to help you with that. The family of one of the victims posted a reward for information leading to her location.

"While the outcome isn't what they'd hoped, they're so grateful they can bury her and move on, that they're prepared to release it to you.

"In the meantime, we'd like your permission to excavate the garden to see if we can locate the missing women."

«« • »»

She sat in a partially obscured seat at the back of the courtroom to watch the judge sentence the man the media dubbed The Pseudonym Killer, because he'd taken a different name as he'd wooed, wed, and killed each one.

Detective Shaw had treated her as a victim rather than an accomplice, but her guilt deepened with each find.

How could she not have known he was killing women and burying them in her garden while she was living with him?

How had she had survived when he killed ten women who looked like her?

Or was it that she looked like them?

She might be invisible to anyone who wasn't looking too hard for her, because the detective helped her close down all her social media accounts, change her name and move away.

Like witness protection, only without being much of a witness, or receiving much protection.

He kept her informed as the police recovered the remains of another four women from her beautiful garden.

It was difficult to bear, but he hadn't shielded her from the details, which made her feel both better and worse about being the lone survivor at the same time.

When the judge read out the sentence of ten consecutive life sentences, without the possibility of parole, she permitted herself a small smile.

And waited to see him escorted from the dock, surrounded by police and security.

Then she waited a little longer as the court emptied around her, until Detective Shaw came and sat next to her.

"Is it over?" she asked.

"Yes. You're free to live a normal life now."

"I'm not sure that my life will ever be normal again."

"Perhaps not, but you owe it to the others to live it well."

"Yes, I suppose I do."

She stood and offered him her hand, "thanks for your help with this."

He stood too, "I'm glad I could help."

She left the room, and before long, was indistinguishable within the crowds.

THE END

ABOUT THE AUTHOR

Alexandria Blaelock writes stories, some of them for *Ellery Queen's Mystery Magazine* and *Pulphouse Fiction Magazine*. She's also written five self-help books applying business techniques to personal matters like getting dressed, cleaning house, and feeding your friends.

She lives in a forest because she enjoys birdsong, the scent of gum leaves and the sun on her face. When not telecommuting to parallel universes from her Melbourne based imagination, she watches K-dramas, talks to animals, and drinks Campari. At the same time.

Discover more at www.alexandriablaelock.com.